Martians Don't Take Temperatures

There are more books about the Bailey School Kids!
Have you read these adventures?

Martians Don't Take Temperatures

by **Debbie Dadey**
and
Marcia Thornton Jones

illustrated by **John Steven Gurney**

A
LITTLE APPLE
PAPERBACK

SCHOLASTIC INC.
New York   Toronto   London   Auckland   Sydney

No part of this publication may be reproduced in whole or in part, or stored in a retrieval system, or transmitted in any form or by any means, electronic, mechanical, photocopying, recording, or otherwise, without written permission of the publisher. For information regarding permission, write to Scholastic Inc., 555 Broadway, New York, NY 10012.

ISBN 0-590-50960-8

12 11 10 9 8 7 6 5 4 3 2 1   6 7 8 9/9 0 1/0

Printed in the U.S.A.   40

First Scholastic printing, January 1996

Book design by Laurie Williams

For Charlene Jones and Ruth Dadey

Contents

1

Windstorm

"We're going to be blown away!" Howie warned Liza, Melody, and Eddie. The four friends had just met under a giant oak tree when a gust of wind whipped through the branches.

"School doesn't start for ten minutes," Eddie griped. "We can't let a little breeze chase us inside."

Liza shivered and zipped up her jacket. "This is no breeze. It's a storm."

"A windstorm," Howie added. "And it's getting stronger."

"Shhh," Melody said with her finger to her lips. "Do you hear that?"

Liza nodded. "It sounds like someone whistling."

Eddie laughed. "That's the wind whistling through your empty skulls."

When Melody reached out to give Eddie a shove, the wind tore her scarf loose. Howie grabbed for it, but the wind snapped the scarf away.

"I'll get it," Eddie said. As he reached for it a huge cloud of red dust swirled across the playground, pushing him into dizzy circles.

"Grab my hand!" Howie screamed with dust blowing all around him. Howie clung to the tree with one hand and reached for Eddie with the other. Eddie caught Howie's hand just as another gust of wind sent all four friends tumbling to the ground.

Melody and Howie covered their eyes and Eddie buried his face in his coat. Liza sneezed so hard her cap popped off her head and blew away.

As suddenly as it began, the wind died

down to a whisper, and then it was gone. The sidewalk was covered with red dust and a fine layer of red coated the bare branches of the oak tree. There was even red dust on the tips of their noses.

"Ah-choo!" Liza sneezed. And then she sneezed again.

"We'd better get inside," Howie said, "before Liza sneezes her head off."

"Cool." Eddie giggled. "I wonder if her head would bounce."

Liza tried to stick her tongue out at Eddie, but she sneezed instead. Melody grabbed Liza's elbow and led her toward the building. They almost bumped into a short, plump woman at the school door.

The woman was feeling around the edges of the door while whistling a strange tune to herself. She bent over and ran her chubby fingers along the bottom of the door. Finally, she took a step backward.

"Open," the stranger said in a stern voice.

Howie looked at Melody and Melody looked at Liza. Liza just sneezed. Eddie started giggling so hard he shook the dust off his nose.

Melody pushed him aside, hoping the stranger didn't notice his laughing. "Welcome to Bailey School," Melody said, pulling open the door.

The stranger stared at the door handle and laughed. "Well, I'll be truttled." Then she disappeared inside.

2

Ah-choo

"You look terrible," Melody told Liza when they were inside the building. The strange woman had scurried away down a side hall.

"So what else is new?" Eddie snickered.

Melody gave Eddie a dirty look. "I mean she looks sick."

Liza sneezed again and rubbed her eyes. "I don't feel very well," she admitted.

"Maybe you should go to the nurse's office and lie down," Howie suggested.

Liza nodded and the four kids headed down the main hall. Melody had her arm around Liza. "Oh, no," Melody said, stopping suddenly. "I forgot. Nurse Smedley retired. There is no school nurse."

7

"Ah-choo!" Liza sneezed and looked as if she were ready to cry.

Howie shrugged his shoulders. "At least she can rest."

The four kids went into the principal's office. The nurse's office was a little room inside the main office.

"Good morning. If it isn't my favorite Bailey School students." Principal Davis waved to them from his big desk.

"Good morning," Melody, Howie, and Eddie said together.

"Ah-choo!" Liza sneezed.

Melody patted Liza on the back. "There was a bad dust storm out on the playground and now Liza feels terrible."

Principal Davis rubbed his bald head and looked at Liza. "Yes," he said, "she does look a little green around the gills."

"She's not a fish," Eddie sputtered.

"That's just a saying," Howie explained. "It means she looks sick."

"Right." Principal Davis nodded. "I think we should see if she has a fever. Why don't you come inside the nurse's office." The four friends followed Principal Davis and watched him put a big glass thermometer in Liza's mouth. He stood beside her and tapped his foot.

"Aren't you supposed to time her?" Melody suggested.

"Oh," Principal Davis said, his bald head turning red. "You're quite right. I think I'm supposed to hold her hand, too."

Principal Davis held Liza's hand, looked at the clock, and tapped his foot. Liza sneezed and held the thermometer in with two fingers.

"Is she done yet?" Eddie asked.

"Let's take a look at it." Principal Davis pulled the thermometer out of Liza's mouth and looked at it.

"I can't tell anything about these

things," Principal Davis confessed.

"Perhaps I can take a look, sir," Howie said softly. Howie wanted to be a doctor and liked to practice whenever he could.

Howie held the thermometer up to the light and squinted. "I think it says 32.4 degrees."

"That means she's dead," Eddie said.

The four kids jumped at a voice behind them. "She's either dead or from outer space."

3

Zot

Standing in the doorway was the same plump woman they had seen at the school door.

She was hardly as tall as Eddie. Her eyelids were smothered with green eyeshadow and she wore a light green pantsuit under a heavy green winter coat. Even her skin and gray hair had a slightly greenish tint.

"No, no," the lady said. "You're doing it all wrong. Let me see that." She took the thermometer from Howie and shook her head. "No wonder you're having trouble. Why, this thing is ancient."

The lady dropped a huge silver suitcase on the floor and started rummaging through it. She held up a green mask and tied it over her mouth. She whistled her strange tune and looked into her suitcase again. "Ah, here we go." The lady held up a big white instrument and stuck it in Liza's ear.

Principal Davis put his hand on the strange lady's arm. "Excuse me," he said, "it's kind of you to help. But who are you and what are you poking in her ear?"

"Maybe she's sucking out Liza's brains." Melody giggled.

"She can't," Eddie explained. "Liza doesn't have any brains."

Liza started to stick her tongue out at Eddie, but she sneezed instead. "Ah-choo! Ah-choo!"

"I'm the new school nurse, Nurse Redding," the lady told them, handing Principal Davis some papers. "And from the look of things, I got here just in the nick of time."

"The dust storm really bothered Liza," Howie explained.

"I can't imagine that," Nurse Redding said. "I love dust. It reminds me of home."

"You must be from the desert," Howie said.

"Or from under my bed." Eddie laughed. "There's plenty of dust there."

"I certainly don't live under your bed!" Nurse Redding said. "I suppose my home would look like a desert to you . . . only it is much colder!"

The thermometer in Liza's ear beeped and Nurse Redding held it up. "Oh, zot! Ninety-nine degrees! This girl is burning with fever!"

"Ah-choo!" Liza sneezed again.

"Let's give you something for that sneeze." Nurse Redding help up a bright green bandage and stuck in on Liza's forehead.

Liza smiled. "When I was a little kid, bandages always made me feel better," she said. "I guess they still do. As a matter of fact, I feel great!"

"Sounds like we have a fantastic new nurse!" Principal Davis said. "You kids better get to class before the bell rings."

Liza, Howie, Melody, and Eddie took off down the hall toward their classroom. Liza skipped beside her friends. "Nurse Redding is great!"

"She's a little strange if you ask me," Eddie said.

"She looks positively green!" Melody squealed.

Eddie giggled. "Maybe she forgot to take a bath this year!"

Liza stopped skipping and put her hands on her hips. "Don't say bad stuff about Nurse Redding! She's the best nurse in the universe!"

"Don't get mad." Howie patted Liza's shoulder. "You have to admit, she is a little different."

"There's nothing wrong with being different," Liza said and stomped off to their classroom.

Eddie looked at his friends. "What got her feathers all ruffled?"

Melody shrugged her shoulders. "I don't know. Maybe Nurse Redding really did suck out her brains."

Eddie and Melody laughed, but Howie whispered silently to himself, "Maybe she did."

4

Normal

"Please put your pencils away," Mrs. Jeepers told her students. Immediately the *click, click, click* of pencils being set down could be heard. The third-graders had been working hard all morning and were ready for a break. Whenever Mrs. Jeepers gave a direction, the kids were sure to follow it. Even Eddie. Most kids were a little afraid of their third-grade teacher. Some even thought she was a vampire.

Mrs. Jeepers glanced at the note in her hands before speaking. "The new Bailey School nurse has sent a message," Mrs. Jeepers said in her Transylvanian accent. "She would like to do a routine checkup on our class at this time."

As the rest of the third-graders hurried to line up, Liza, Melody, Howie, and Eddie gathered at the end of the line. "I have a strange feeling about this nurse," Howie whispered to his friends.

Liza smiled. "You should have some of her wonderful bandages. Then you wouldn't feel bad about anything! I've never felt better in my life!"

Eddie poked Liza in the arm. "You feel the same to me! Icky!"

Howie stepped between Eddie and Liza. "This is no time to be silly. I think we have a serious problem. And her name is Nurse Redding."

"What are you talking about?" Melody asked. "You don't even know Nurse Redding."

Howie looked around to make sure no one was listening. Then he spoke very softly. "I know she appeared during a dust storm, and Bailey City never has

dust storms in the middle of winter."

"That doesn't mean anything," Liza blurted out.

"But Nurse Redding has super-duper bandages and thermometers. Things that no one else has ever heard of," Howie told them.

"She's just on the cutting edge of medicine," Melody said.

"Then why didn't Nurse Redding know how to open a door?" Howie asked. "If she's a normal nurse then she should be smart enough to know how to open a door. Not unless . . ."

"Unless what?" Eddie asked.

"Unless Nurse Redding isn't a normal nurse," Howie said slowly as the rest of the class filed out the door.

5

Gravity

The four friends hurried to the office and crowded into Nurse Redding's room. Mrs. Jeepers had already left the class with the new nurse.

"These records are ancient," the new nurse was saying. Her voice was loud and flat. "We must flebble them."

Carey, a girl with bouncy curls, raised her hand. "What does flebble mean?"

Nurse Redding pulled on her green mask and peered at Carey. "Flebble? It is just my way of saying to fix something."

"I'd like to flebble that nurse," Eddie whispered.

"Shhh," Liza warned.

First, Nurse Redding made Melody stand at the far end of the room and

23

read from a chart. The chart had strange shapes on it.

"I can't read that," Melody said.

"Oh, zot," Nurse Redding said. "You will need eyeglasses."

"I can see it," Melody interrupted. "I just can't read it."

"The chart doesn't make sense," Liza said kindly. "We're used to reading letters."

Nurse Redding looked confused. "But those are letters."

"They aren't any letters we've seen before," Howie blurted. He rummaged through a nearby closet, pulling out an old yellow poster. "Here's the chart the other nurse used. It has letters on it we can read."

Nurse Redding stared at the poster for a full minute before smiling. "Of course, how silly of me!" she said.

Melody and the rest of the class had no

trouble reading from the old poster.

After checking their eyesight, Nurse Redding measured every third-grader. She whistled her funny whistle as she worked.

"How many feet am I?" Eddie asked. Nurse Redding blinked twice before answering, "Two."

"I am not," Eddie sputtered.

"Of course you are," Nurse Redding argued. "All of you have two feet. Unless some of you are hiding a few."

Most of the kids giggled, but not Howie. He was totally serious when he tapped Nurse Redding on the shoulder. "Eddie wants to know how tall he is."

"Why didn't he just say so?" Nurse Redding glanced at her chart. "Eddie is exactly six schlepits and twelve nypto-fractions. Now, let's get everyone's weight."

"What's a schlepit?" Melody asked

softly while Nurse Redding helped Carey up on the scale.

Eddie shrugged. "I have no idea. Maybe we should pay more attention during math class."

Nobody heard Eddie because just then Nurse Redding gasped. "This cannot be right!" she said. "Someone else try."

This time, Howie got on the scale. Nurse Redding put her nose right up to the scale. "How can this be?" she asked. "This machine must be broken."

"I don't think so," Liza said. "It always worked before."

Nurse Redding helped Howie down. "I know how to check it," she said. "I shall weigh myself. After all, I know how much I weigh."

Nurse Redding climbed aboard the scale and checked the readout. Then she let out a blood-curdling scream.

"What's wrong?" Howie asked.

"I've never weighed this much in my life," Nurse Redding moaned.

Melody patted her shoulder. "It's all right. My mom says gravity does strange things to women as they get older."

Nurse Redding stopped moaning and looked at Melody. Then Nurse Redding smiled. "Of course! That's it! Gravity!"

Liza rushed up with a cup of water. "This might make you feel better," she said.

Nurse Redding looked at the liquid in the cup before asking, "What is this?"

Liza giggled. "It's just water. I thought you might be thirsty."

"Water?" Nurse Redding asked. "Of course, thank you." Nurse Redding sniffed the water and then slowly drank it.

"I remember what I wanted to tell you all," Nurse Redding said. "Water is essential to human development. Humans should drink at least eight glasses of water every day. Even if it is so wet." Nurse Redding giggled.

"How else would water be?" Eddie asked.

Nurse Redding didn't answer because Mrs. Jeepers came back into the room. "Class," Mrs. Jeepers said, "we must leave now. It is time for science."

"All right," Howie said. "I love studying about the solar system."

Mrs. Jeepers smiled an odd little half-smile at Nurse Redding. "Thank you for checking the class. It is very nice to have you at Bailey Elementary."

Nurse Redding nodded to Mrs. Jeepers. "This school is wonderful. As a matter of fact, it is out of this world!"

6

Marshmallows

After school, Howie grabbed Eddie's arm. They were under the big oak tree on the playground with Melody and Liza.

"I have to tell you something," Howie said seriously. "It might scare you."

Eddie laughed. "Nothing you say can scare me."

"You may change your mind," Howie said.

"Just tell us," Melody told Howie.

"Okay," Howie said slowly. "You know all the strange measurements and funny words Nurse Redding uses?"

Liza nodded. "It's almost like she's from another country."

"Or another planet," Howie whispered.

"What?" Liza, Eddie, and Melody said together.

Howie took a deep breath and looked at his friends. "I think Nurse Redding is from Mars."

Eddie and Liza burst out laughing, but Melody twisted her ponytail.

"She did look as if she'd never seen water before," Melody said slowly.

"That's because there is no water on Mars," Howie said. "Don't you remember that from science?"

Melody jumped up and down. "I remember that Mars is called the Red Planet."

"So what?" Eddie said.

Melody rolled her eyes. "Don't you get it? Nurse *Red*-ding? I bet she is from Mars!"

"You guys are crazy," Liza said. "Names don't mean anything. I guess you think that marshmallows are from outer space,

too, just because they start with *mars*."

"Your brains are full of marshmallows," Eddie snickered.

"All right," Howie said. "If you're so smart, just follow me. Then we'll see who has marshmallows for brains!"

The kids were so busy rushing after Howie that none of them heard the strange whistling noise that floated across the Bailey School playground.

7

Martian Madness

Howie didn't slow down until he reached the corner of Green Street and Smith Lane. Then Howie stopped so quickly Eddie ran right into him.

"Why did you stop?" Eddie snapped.

Howie pointed to the small sign by the sidewalk. "Because I plan on catching a bus and this is the nearest stop," Howie told them.

"A bus?" Melody asked. "To where?"

"The planetarium," Howie answered.

Eddie laughed so hard he had to gasp for breath. "I always knew you were nuts! Now you're going to a place where they help crazy people."

Liza tapped Eddie on the arm. "You shouldn't call people crazy. It's not nice."

Howie shook his head. "Besides, I'm talking about a planetarium, not a sanitarium. A planetarium is where they study the sky and outer space."

Eddie laughed even harder. "That's even better because you have plenty of space between your ears."

"Laugh all you want," Howie snapped. "But you'll be sorry when you find out I'm right."

Eddie leaned against the bus stop sign. "I've already learned enough today," he argued. "I shouldn't have to learn anything unless I'm at school."

"If we want to find out the truth about Nurse Redding, we better do what Howie says," Melody interrupted.

"Don't tell me you believe this Martian madness," Liza asked her friend.

Melody shrugged. "I am a little scared. What Howie says makes sense."

Liza shook a finger in front of Melody's

nose. "How could you believe Nurse Redding is a Martian? She's a fantastic nurse, but that's all."

"I don't know what to believe," Melody said slowly. "Going to the planetarium will help us decide what to do."

"Well, if we're going, we'd better run home and get permission first," Liza suggested.

Howie nodded. "Okay, we'll meet back here in a half hour to catch the next bus."

An hour later the four kids were standing in front of the giant planetarium.

"I hope you know what you're doing," Eddie said.

Howie looked at his best friend. "Not yet. But we'll find out what to do here at the Bailey City Planetarium."

Howie led his friends up the long sidewalk and into the planetarium. Inside, the building was dark and quiet. Liza felt

like she should whisper. "What are we looking for?"

Howie pointed to a sign. "That show would be a good place to start," he told her. "A movie is getting ready to begin."

The four friends filed into the huge auditorium and sat in big comfortable chairs that leaned way back so they could stare at the ceiling. As soon as they sat down, the lights dimmed and loud music boomed from the speakers. The ceiling became the red planet of Mars. Soon Howie, Melody, Eddie, and Liza felt like they were plummeting through space.

Liza whimpered and Howie gripped the arms of his chair. "Hang on," Eddie said. "It looks like we're going into orbit."

8

Invasion

"Wow," Eddie whispered. "That was the best movie I ever saw!" The show had just finished, but the four friends still gripped the arms of their chairs.

"It felt like we were really hurtling through space," Liza agreed. "It's hard to believe we've been sitting here instead of zooming around Mars."

"We're lucky we don't live on Mars," Melody said. "It's so cold."

"And dry," Howie added. "The only water is underground and frozen."

Melody nodded. "That's why it's the Red Planet. It's so dry the wind swirls up huge dust clouds so the entire planet looks red."

"But we'd never have to worry about

getting fat on Mars." Eddie laughed. "No gravity makes everything weigh less."

Howie's eyes were as big as flying saucers. "Don't you get it? Nurse Redding forgot about gravity making her weigh more on Earth. That's why she got so upset when she climbed on those scales."

"If eating too many sugar cookies makes our new school nurse a Martian," Eddie argued, "then Principal Davis must be the king of Mars."

"But Principal Davis didn't just appear in a cloud of swirling dust," Melody told Eddie. "And he isn't surprised at how wet water is."

"It all makes sense," Howie said in a whisper. "Nurse Redding really is a Martian."

Liza shook her head. "I'm pretty sure Martians don't work at schools as nurses. And they definitely don't use bandages

or take temperatures. Besides, that movie said there's no life on Mars."

"That's right," Melody squealed, "because now the Martians are right here in Bailey City. But what do they want from us? Do you think they want our brains?"

Eddie laughed. "Then they definitely came to the wrong place."

"Maybe they're just vacationing," Melody suggested.

"Nobody vacations in Bailey City," Eddie argued.

"Bailey City is a perfectly nice place to visit," Liza told Eddie. "It's sure a lot nicer than that dust bowl of a planet."

Howie grabbed Liza's arm. "That's it, Liza," Howie gasped. "You figured out why the Martians have invaded Bailey City."

Liza pulled away from Howie. "What are you talking about? I didn't say anything about Martians. I just said Bailey City is a great place to live."

Howie nodded. "And that's exactly why the Martians have invaded. They're taking over Bailey City!"

9

Help

"You guys are scaring me," Liza whimpered.

"There's nothing to be scared of," Eddie told her. "These guys are totally wrong. Nurse Redding is a little weird, but she's no Martian."

"Shhh," Melody hissed. "There she is."

The four kids heard Nurse Redding's strange whistling before they saw her. No one said a word as she walked past them into the movie theater.

"What's she doing here?" Melody whispered.

"Let's watch her," Howie suggested.

Liza shook her finger. "We shouldn't do that," she said. "That's spying."

Eddie grinned. "Then let's do it."

Liza sighed, but followed her friends to the theater door. The four kids peered around the corner of the door and gasped.

Nurse Redding was leaning back in one of the chairs and staring at the ceiling. There was a big smile on her face and, in the low light of the planetarium, her skin looked greener than ever. She didn't even notice the four kids staring at her from the doorway.

"What's she doing?" Eddie asked.

"Shhh," Howie warned, "she might hear you."

Melody pulled her friends away from the door and whispered, "I bet she's watching the movie because she's homesick."

"Of course," Howie agreed. "The movie is so real, it makes her think she's back on Mars."

Eddie shook his head. "You guys have been in orbit a little too long."

Liza started to agree with Eddie, but a uniformed worker came up to the kids. "How did you like the Mars movie?" the worker asked.

"It was great!" Eddie told him. "I could see it every day."

The worker chuckled and pointed toward Nurse Redding. "You'd be like that lady there. She came in yesterday to watch the movie and stayed all evening. She's already seen the show four times and now she's back again."

Melody's eyes got wide and she spoke slowly. "She must really like Mars."

The worker laughed again. "If I didn't know better, I'd think she was from Mars." The man waved to them and went into the theater to start the movie. The door closed behind him with a thud.

"Did you hear that?" Howie said. "He thinks Nurse Redding is a Martian, too!"

"He was just kidding," Liza told her friends.

Howie started walking toward the outside door. "Well, I'm not kidding. We have to do something and we have to do it now!"

10

F.A.T.S.

"Now where are you going?" Eddie asked Howie as they raced down the sidewalk in front of the planetarium.

"We'd better go home," Liza told him. "We have homework to do."

Howie stopped running and pointed next door to the Federal Aeronautics Technology Station where his dad worked. The huge building was totally surrounded by a tall wire fence. "This will only take a few minutes," Howie said. "I want to ask my dad what we should do."

"I know what we should do," Eddie told him. "We should play video games."

Liza put her hands on her hips. "No,

we should forget about Mars and go do our homework."

Howie looked seriously at his friends. "The safety of Bailey City is worth ten minutes of your precious time."

"Oh, all right," Eddie said, rolling his eyes. "Let's get this over with."

Howie marched up to a small post and pushed a big button. Static exploded from the little black speaker perched on top of the post.

"May I help you?" a woman's voice boomed from the box.

"It's Howie Jones. I'm here to see my dad."

"Please follow the drive to the front door," the voice said. Slowly the tall gates beside the post swung open. As soon as the four friends slipped inside, the gates clanged shut.

A woman in a long white lab coat met

them at the front door and led them to Howie's dad's office. Dr. Jones was working on his computer. He looked just like Howie, only bigger and with gold-rimmed glasses. "Hi, kids," Dr. Jones said. "What can I do for you?"

"Howie thinks we have Martians here in Bailey City!" Eddie blurted out.

Dr. Jones smiled. "Who knows? Maybe there really are beings from other planets."

Liza gasped and Howie shook his head. "No, we're serious," he said. "We think our new school nurse may be from Mars."

"And we need to know how to save the city from her," Melody explained.

Dr. Jones pushed his glasses back up on his nose. "I'm not too sure there are such things as Martians."

"See, I told you so," Liza said, folding her arms in front of her chest.

"But," Dr. Jones continued, "if we were being invaded by Martians, there's one way we could get rid of them."

"How?" Melody, Howie, and Eddie asked together.

Dr. Jones smiled and took his glasses off. "Gather 'round and I'll tell you."

11

Zlapiteed

"Do you think Howie will try out his dad's plan?" Melody asked.

It was early the next morning and Eddie and Melody were waiting on the playground for Howie and Liza. A cold wind rattled the bare branches of their favorite oak tree. Melody hugged her jacket tight and Eddie stuffed his hands deep into his pockets.

"A little warm weather wouldn't scare off a real Martian," Eddie said. "Besides, Howie's too smart to try his dad's silly plan."

"That's what worries me," Melody said seriously. "Howie's the smartest kid I know and he believes Nurse Redding is a Martian."

"If he's right, Nurse Redding must feel right at home in this cold weather," Eddie joked.

"Shh," Melody warned. "I think we're about to find out."

Long before Nurse Redding came into view, Eddie and Melody heard her strange whistled tune. The two friends peeked around the fat trunk of the oak tree to watch her as she rounded the corner of Bailey Elementary.

"Look at that," Eddie whispered. "She's not even wearing a coat today."

"It's just like Howie said," Melody squeaked. "Nobody but a Martian could be that happy in this cold wind."

"Why are you standing out here?" Eddie asked. "You must be a Martian, too."

"Am not!" Melody snapped.

"Then let's go inside," Eddie said. "We can follow Howie's Martian and see what she's up to."

"What about Howie and Liza?" Melody asked. "Aren't we going to wait for them?"

"They're smart enough to find their way across the playground." Eddie could tell by the way Melody shivered in the icy wind that she wouldn't argue. He led the way across the playground and into the building.

"Where did she go?" Eddie asked Melody.

Melody shrugged. "Maybe she went into the cafeteria for a Moon-Pie breakfast."

Eddie and Melody made their way through the halls of Bailey Elementary to the cafeteria. Sure enough, Nurse Redding was eating breakfast with a group of Bailey kids.

"Let's get closer," Melody said, but a girl with blonde curls got there before them. Carey plopped down next to Nurse Redding and sniffed.

"Sounds like you're coming down with something," Nurse Redding told Carey.

Carey nodded so hard her curly hair bounced. "I feel awful."

"Come with me," Nurse Redding said. "I know just the thing to make you all flebbled again."

Nurse Redding handed her tray to Eddie. "Please deposit my tray to be cleaned," she asked. Then she marched out of the cafeteria with Carey.

Eddie stared at the tray in his hands and gasped. Nurse Redding's plate was half-covered with green cheese. "Howie was right!" he said. "Only a Martian from outer space would eat green cheese."

"Hurry! We have to save Carey," Melody said. Eddie turned the tray in and darted after Melody to the nurse's office.

Carey almost bumped into them when she skipped out of Nurse Redding's small

office. On her forehead was a bright green bandage.

"Hi, Eddie and Melody," Carey said happily. "Did you come to see the nurse?"

"No," Melody said. "We came to make sure you were okay."

Carey batted her long eyelashes and grinned. "Me? Why, I feel great. As a matter of fact, I'm just zlapiteed!" Then Carey skipped down the hall.

12

Heat Wave

"Good morning, kids," Principal Davis said to Melody and Howie. "Did Nurse Redding get you all flebbled up?" Principal Davis had a bright green bandage right on top of his bald head.

Melody didn't say anything, just nodded and rushed away from the office. Eddie followed her and they stopped around the first corner. "We've got to do something!"

Melody hissed. "Nurse Redding is taking over the whole school. She even has Principal Davis under her control!"

"What are you guys talking about?" Liza asked from behind them.

Eddie grabbed Liza on the shoulder. "We know you like Nurse Redding, but we think Howie is right. Nurse Redding is a Martian."

Liza rolled her eyes. "I'll believe that when I see her fly out of here on a spaceship."

Just then Nurse Redding rushed by and burst out the back door.

"What was that all about?" Melody asked.

Liza and Eddie shrugged, but Howie laughed out loud from behind them. Liza, Eddie, and Melody turned to see a very different-looking Howie.

"What's with you and Nurse Redding?" Liza asked.

Eddie giggled. "You look like a berserk beach bum."

Howie was dressed in sandals, shorts, a flowered shirt, straw hat, and green sunglasses. He was carrying his backpack and a beach umbrella.

"Maybe so," Howie said. "But it worked. Nurse Redding practically flew out of here when I told her a heat wave was on the way."

"That proves it," Melody said. "She really is a Martian."

"That doesn't prove any ..." Liza started to say before she was interrupted by a terrible whistling noise from outside the school.

"What is that?" Eddie asked and pulled open a door.

"Don't!" Howie shouted, but he was too late. Eddie had already opened the door. A huge gust of wind tore into the school and knocked the kids against the wall.

"Help!" Liza screamed as dust flew all around her. "The Martians are coming!"

In an instant, the wind stopped and a fine red powder settled all over the kids and the hallway. "Yuck," Liza said, sneezing. "This stuff is awful."

Melody put her hands on her hips and looked at Liza. "I thought you didn't believe in Martians."

"That's right," Eddie said. "You were screaming that the Martians were coming."

Liza turned red and shrugged. "I didn't know what I was saying."

"Everything's all right now," Howie said. "The only Martian around here is gone now." The four kids looked out the open door at the playground. Red dust covered everything in sight, including the oak tree.

"I guess Nurse Redding really is gone," Melody said.

"Yes," Principal Davis said from behind them. "It's true. Bailey City's climate didn't agree with her. It's no wonder with all these crazy dust storms and now I hear there's talk of a heat wave." Principal Davis walked away, shaking his head and pulling the green bandage from his forehead.

"You know what that means," Liza said.

"What?" Melody, Howie, and Eddie asked.

Liza giggled. "It means everything at Bailey Elementary is all flebbled up!"

Debbie Dadey and Marcia Thornton Jones have fun writing stories together. When they both worked at an elementary school in Lexington, Kentucky, Debbie was the school librarian and Marcia was a teacher. During their lunch break in the school cafeteria, they came up with the idea of the Bailey School kids.

Recently Debbie and her family moved to Aurora, Illinois. Marcia and her husband still live in Kentucky where she continues to teach. How do these authors still write together? They talk on the phone and use computers and fax machines!

LITTLE  APPLE®

*T*here are fun times ahead with kids just like you in Little Apple books! Once you take a bite out of a Little Apple—you'll want to read more!

Reading Excitement for Kids with BIG Appetites!

☐ NA42833-0 **Catwings** Ursula K. LeGuin $2.95

☐ NA42832-2 **Catwings Return** Ursula K. LeGuin $2.95

☐ NA41821-1 **Class Clown** Johanna Hurwitz $2.75

☐ NA43868-9 **The Haunting of Grade Three**
Grace Maccarone $2.75

☐ NA40966-2 **Rent A Third Grader** B.B. Hiller $2.99

☐ NA41944-7 **The Return of the Third Grade Ghost Hunters**
Grace Maccarone $2.75

☐ NA44477-8 **Santa Claus Doesn't Mop Floors**
Debra Dadey and Marcia Thornton Jones $2.99

☐ NA42031-3 **Teacher's Pet** Johanna Hurwitz $2.99

☐ NA43411-X **Vampires Don't Wear Polka Dots**
Debra Dadey and Marcia Thornton Jones $2.99

☐ NA44061-6 **Werewolves Don't Go to Summer Camp**
Debra Dadey and Marcia Thornton Jones $2.99

Available wherever you buy books...or use the coupon below.

SCHOLASTIC INC., Box 7502, 2931 East McCarty Street, Jefferson City, MO 65102

Please send me the books I have checked above. I am enclosing $ _____ (please add $2.00 to cover shipping and handling). Send check or money order—no cash or C.O.D.s please.

Name _____

Address _____

City _____ State/Zip _____

Please allow four to six weeks for delivery. Offer good in the U.S.A. only. Sorry, mail orders are not available to residents of Canada. Prices subject to change.

LA595